This book belongs to:

....

....

....

Retold by Gaby Goldsack
Illustrated by Ruth Galloway (Advocate)
Designed by Jester Designs

Language consultant: Betty Root

ISBN 1-84461-209-0

Marks and Spencer p.l.c.
PO Box 3339, Chester CH99 9QS
www.marksandspencer.com

Copyright © Exclusive Editions 2002

Printed in China

Goldilocks
and the
Three Bears

Helping Your Child to Read

Learning to read is an exciting challenge for most children. From a very early age, sharing story books with children, talking about the pictures and guessing what might happen next are all very important parts of the reading experience.

Sharing reading

Set aside a regular quiet time to share reading with younger children, or to be on hand to encourage older children as they develop into independent readers.

First Readers are intended to encourage and support the early stages of learning to read. They present well-loved tales that children will happily listen to again and again. Familiarity helps children to identify some of the words and phrases.

When you feel your child is ready to move on a little, encourage them to join in so that you read the story aloud together. Always pause to talk about the pictures. The easy-to-read speech bubbles in **First Readers** provide an excellent 'joining-in' activity. The bright, clear illustrations and matching text will help children to understand the story.

Building confidence

In time, children will want to read *to* you. When this happens, be patient and give continual praise. They may not read all the words correctly, but children's substitutions are often very good guesses.

The repetition in each book is particularly helpful for building confidence. If your child cannot read a particular word, go back to the beginning of the sentence and read it together so the meaning is not lost. Most importantly, do not continue if your child is tired or simply in need of a change.

Reading alone

The next step is for your child to read alone. Try to be on hand to give help and support. Remember to give lots of encouragement and praise.

Together with other simple stories, **First Readers** will ensure that children will find reading an enjoyable and rewarding experience.

Once upon a time there were three
bears. They lived in a little house
in a big wood.

There was great big Daddy Bear.

I'm big.

Then there
was middle-sized
Mummy Bear.

I'm middle
sized.

I'm just
little.

And there was
tiny little
Baby Bear.

One day, Mummy Bear made porridge.

She put some in a great big bowl.

She put some in a middle-sized bowl.

And she put some in a tiny little bowl.

The porridge was too hot to eat.
The three bears went for a walk
while it cooled down.

Not far away, a little girl was also walking in the big wood. The little girl had golden hair. She was called Goldilocks.

Is anyone home?

Soon Goldilocks found the house of the three bears. The door was wide open.

Goldilocks walked right into the house.
She saw the bowls of porridge. She
tasted some from the great big bowl.
It was too salty.

She tasted some from the middle-sized
bowl. It was too sweet.

She tasted some from the tiny little bowl.
It was just right. Goldilocks ate it all up!

Then Goldilocks saw three chairs.
She sat in the great big chair. It was
too high.

She sat in the middle-sized chair. It was
too low.

She sat in the tiny little chair. It was
just right.

Crack! Oh no, it wasn't! Goldilocks
was too heavy. The tiny little chair
broke into pieces.

Next Goldilocks went upstairs.

She lay on the great big bed. It was too hard.

She lay on the middle-sized bed. It was too soft.

She lay on the tiny little bed. It was just right, and Goldilocks fell asleep.

Soon the three bears came home.

"Who's been eating my porridge?"
asked Daddy Bear in a great big voice.

"Who's been eating my porridge?" asked
Mummy Bear in a middle-sized voice.

"Who's been eating my porridge, and eaten it all up?" asked Baby Bear in a tiny little voice.

Then the three bears saw their chairs.
"Who's been sitting in my chair?" asked
Daddy Bear in a great big voice.

"Who's been sitting in my chair?" asked
Mummy Bear in a middle-sized voice.

"Who's been sitting in my chair and broken it?" asked Baby Bear in a tiny little voice.

Then the three bears went upstairs.
"Who's been sleeping in my bed?" asked
Daddy Bear in a great big voice.

"Who's been sleeping in my bed?" asked
Mummy Bear in a middle-sized voice.

"Who's been sleeping in my bed?" asked Baby Bear in a tiny little voice. "And she's still here!"

Just then, Goldilocks woke up. When
she saw the three bears, she was scared.

Goldilocks jumped up and rushed down
the stairs. Then she ran out of the house.

The three bears did not see Goldilocks ever again.

Read and Say

How many of these words can you say? The pictures will help you. Look back in your book and see if you can find the words in the story.

bed

Baby Bear

bowl

chair

Daddy Bear

Goldilocks

door

house

Mummy Bear

wood

Titles in this series, subject to availability: